Goodnight Pablo

Pablo created by Gráinne Mc Guinness
Written by Andrew Brenner and Sumita Majumdar

LADYBIRD BOOKS

UK | USA | Canada | Ireland | Australia | India | New Zealand | South Africa

Ladybird Books is part of the Penguin Random House group of companies
whose addresses can be found at global.penguinrandomhouse.com.

www.penguin.co.uk   www.puffin.co.uk   www.ladybird.co.uk

Penguin
Random House
UK

First published 2020
001

PAPER OWL FILMS

Printed in China

A CIP catalogue record for this book is available from the British Library

ISBN: 978-0-241-41524-5

All correspondence to:
Ladybird Books
Penguin Random House Children's
80 Strand, London WC2R 0RL

FSC
www.fsc.org

MIX
Paper from
responsible sources
FSC® C018179

Tang

Noa

Draff

I'm Pablo!

Llama

Mouse   Wren

These are my friends, the Book Animals!
The Book Animals live in the Art World,
where I draw my stories.

It was nearly the time of day when the colours change — the time that Mum tells me to go to bed. I **was** in bed, but I didn't want to sleep . . .

. . . so I started to draw a story.

I drew everything **blue** – deep, dark blue –
the deep, dark blue that makes it hard to see.

"Hello? Mouse? Are you there?"
called Wren.

"Is Mouse where?" called Mouse.

"Are you there?" asked Wren.

"No," said Mouse. "I'm here!"

The blue was **so blue** that
Mouse and Wren kept bumping
into each other.

"Sorry, Mouse," said Wren.
"Everything is hard to see at **blue**,
when the colours change."

"At blue?" said Mouse.
"You mean at **night**!"

"No! No!" said Wren. "Don't say that word. If you say that word, it means you have to go to sleep! And if you go to sleep, then you **disappear!**"

"Going to sleep means you shut your
eyes so your body can have a rest,"
said Mouse.

"You disappear," insisted Wren.
"Everybody **disappears**!"

"That's not true," said Mouse. "Nobody disappears. If we did, we wouldn't be here in the morning."

But Wren kept on flapping around the room.

"It must be true!" Wren said.
"Look! All our friends are gone!"

I couldn't see the rest of the
Book Animals either . . .

. . . until Wren flew into the lamp by accident.
Suddenly, the blue got bright and Noasaurus woke up.

"I was sleeping," said Noa. It's ni—"
"Don't say it!" cried Wren.

Wren flapped her wings
even more, and Draff
and Llama woke up, too.

"See," said Mouse. "Nobody has
disappeared. Everybody's here."

"I'm definitely here," said Draff.

"I'm definitely here," said Noa.

"I'm definitely here," repeated Llama.

"But I don't see Tang anywhere,"
I said, looking around.

"**Oh no!** Tang's disappeared!"
cried Wren, flapping and flapping.
"He's **really, really disappeared!**"

"Found him!" said Noa. "He's sleeping."
"Mouse needs to sleep, too," said Mouse, with a very big yawn.
"I don't need to sleep!" said Wren.
"In point of fact, **everybody** needs to sleep," said Draff.

Everyone tried to go to sleep, but I carried on drawing.
The blue got brighter . . . and brighter . . . and brighter!
"Pablo! What are you doing?" asked Draff.

"I'm drawing an **Always Sun**," I said,
"so it will always be shining."
"And it will never be blue again?"
asked Wren, looking happy.
"**Never**!" I told her.

The Always Sun smiled, lighting up the whole room!
But not everyone was smiling.
"Pablo! It's **bright**," complained Mouse.

"And we don't usually have the sun **inside** the house!" said Draff.

"Much too bright for sleeping!" agreed Noa.

"OK. OK," I said, as Noa helped me push the Always Sun out of the window.

But it was still very bright, even with sunglasses. So we made it smaller and smaller and smaller . . .

. . . until it was just a tiny bit of light in the sky.
"Now it just looks like a star," I said sadly.

"In point of fact, the sun **is** a
star, Pablo," explained Draff.

It was a beautiful star.

I kept thinking about the Always Star.
It made me feel sparkly.

The lights went off, and everything went
blue – deep, dark blue – the deep,
dark blue that makes it hard to see . . .

. . . but this time
the blue felt calm.

"I can't see you now,"
said Wren. "Mouse?"

"Mouse is still here," said Mouse.

"I'm here, too," said Noa.

"So am I," said Draff.

"I'm definitely here," said Llama.

Tang was making a funny
sleeping noise. We knew
Tang was there!

"What about Pablo?" asked Wren.
"Pablo didn't say he was here!"

I was still there. But I was too sleepy to say so.
"Pablo's still here," said Mouse. "He hasn't disappeared."
"Oh! But how?" asked Wren.

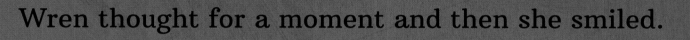
Wren thought for a moment and then she smiled.

"Maybe he has a light on . . .
on the inside," she said.

"Maybe he does," Mouse agreed.

Even in the **blue**, Wren knew I was there.

She felt calm and could finally sleep . . .
and I could go to sleep, too.

"Goodnight, Wren," said Mouse.
"See you in the morning."
"See you in the morning," said Wren,
"after the blue."